Praise for

"The poems that make Madeline Troscl[...] generous geography that exists, because we're in it: 'meet me at the eage. [...] waiting, and we'll be moving.' The swamps, wetlands, and bayous Trosclair-Rotolo writes are alive and always in the middle of their own conversation with the storms and seasons. Like no other collection I've read, *Bottomlands* tells us to be a part of this world is to stake yourself in both the beauty and precarity, on the edge of the greatest mercy where 'Nothing is quite yet lost.'"

—C. T. Salazar, author of *Headless John the Baptist Hitchhiking*

"South Louisiana is a confluence—of land and water, of fresh and salt, of cultures, of foods, of music, of life and loss, past and present, hope and pain. It's a rich, brackish cradle unlike any other homeland you could imagine. With clarity and great beauty, Madeline Trosclair-Rotolo's *Bottomlands* captures all of it as well as any collection of poetry I've ever read. Oysters, Spoonbills, storm winds, home generators, crab traps, Magnalite pots, family, memories, and the water that makes our world—it's all here glowing with truth and marking place like a buoy against the horizon line. Drop anchor and stay for a spell. Cast your line amongst this book's bounty. I guarantee the catch will be worth your time."

—Jack B. Bedell, author of *Against the Woods' Dark Trunks*
Poet Laureate, State of Louisiana, 2017–2019

"In her evocative debut collection, Madeline Trosclair-Rotolo's poems place the reader in her native Gulf coast. These poems situate the reader into the cyclical rolling over of one storm season to the next, between destruction and reconstruction. They are the median of Interstate 10 during a storm evacuation as people traffic to and from their homes east and west between hope and fear. The poems are 'an endless stream / of hot gulf air awaiting a name.' And, in the end, this debut collection itself is a kind of hurricane with its own power to tear down its reader, to dissemble with the gust of each line break. But like the people and communities in this book, the storm of these poems engenders moments of healing. They don't promise that the breaking will end, only that what is broken and built again will be stronger than before. If we travel to Rome, we can read the gravestone of John Keats that says, 'Here lies one whose name is writ in water.' If you open the pages of *Bottomlands*, you'll find a poet who, in water, has written the people and places that she calls home."

—Cody Smith, author of *Gulf* and *Delta Summers*

BOTTOMLANDS

Poems

Madeline
Trosclair–Rotolo

BELLE
POINT
PRESS

Fort Smith, Arkansas

B
O
T
T
O
M
L
A
N
D
S

BOTTOMLANDS

Cover image © JillianSuzanne via Canva Pro License
Author photograph © Michelle Gomez

Edited by Casie Dodd
Design & typography by Belle Point Press

Belle Point Press, LLC
Fort Smith, Arkansas
bellepointpress.com
editor@bellepointpress.com

Find Belle Point Press
on Facebook,
Twitter (@BellePointPress),
and Instagram (@bellepointpress)

Printed in the United States of America

27 26 25 24 23   1 2 3 4 5

Library of Congress Control Number: 2023931919

ISBN: 978-1-960215-01-7

TBL/BPP12

Dedicated to family.
Couldn't have done this without the love I have been shown.

Dedicated to friends, good timers, & fellow swamp rats.

I love each of y'all.

CONTENTS

UNTITLED

A land. A water. Where freshwater kisses meet the salt. A sponge. The space in between where horizon lines tantalize dark clouds and winds rage differently here. A bottomland so soft born of the sodden earth. This is where we get stuck. This is where our bodies lie. A truth. An inevitable washing away where only so much can stay behind to bear witness. A buffer. To bear witness to loss. The ones who stay behind when the land doesn't love you back anymore know the hurt. We all know the hurt. A land that is hurting. Actively. Sharply. Both habit and habitat. Inhabitants celebrate differently here. Booze poured out for the blessing of the fleet. A shot downed to ease storm season anxiety. Brown water. Grey land. Blue black sky. Where grasses bluesed across water. Softened silt falls off the shelf. A song. A prayer. The rosary sank to bottom. Cargo > meets waves > meets open water > meet me at the edge. I'll be waiting, and we'll be moving. We have no choice but to move. Do not confuse this with not having a choice. There were choices made here. A land. A water. A mixing. A meeting.

ATLANTIC HEATING UP,
TROPICAL STORM EXPECTED

But it is unclear whether she will threaten
land gone from last year's floods. After
a drowsy beginning, water wakes up
stretching its musseled limbs against oil rigs.

Today is the anniversary when you were still here,
when I was a kid and you hit hard, when
everyone stood and watched cities fishbowl.

Today is the anniversary you did not know where
you were, and I slept on a blowup mattress in the living
room because upstairs was too far away
while others prayed in the attic.

On the roof of God's house people are air lifted away.
On the roof of God's house is a blue tarp.

DELTA

August sparks electricity
where each touch is heat lightning in
every nerve like a tugboat in a bayou.
A tin can in battered waves with
a storm that barrels toward the Gulf.
Nameless and heat stricken with a
don't-walk-on-the-blacktop hot
and Dad-doesn't-cut-the-grass real hot.
Fingertips burn three months
out the year and   I am an endless stream

of hot gulf air awaiting a name. I eat away
the edges of myself, whittling away coastlines
until all of my flesh fits within
the confines of an eye. That sweet spot
of lucidity—a knowing of where I have been
and where I am headed.

Down and only
to drown you.

FOUNDED IN FRESHWATER,
BIRTHED TO THE BRACKISH

I belong in the delta, my
heart in a daiquiri cup

cast within a nameless
waters' muck and no Bayou

St. Blank decomposing it.
I think I offend such spaces

with its swarming gnats on
the path and termite season

stuck in my pocket. Too
much flesh, too much color

lacking of the browns and grays—
my edges not quite yellowing.

Founded in freshwater
and these levees break

me. Algae, algae soaking up
the sun, fish floating belly up.

LAMENT FOR THE RIVER'S LOSS

I remember the molar in my mouth with its now empty pocket.
I remember the island at the river's mouth—brown water pools in its absence.
I remember the largeness of the Tchefuncte's basin.
I remember my smallness.
I remember seeing everything as bigger than its true size.
I remember my mother telling me I make category fives out of 3pm storms.
I remember baited shrimp drying on wooden docks.
I remember fearing crab gills.
I remember Capri cigarettes.
I remember finding the edge of the world inside myself.
I remember purple August skies dotted with egrets.
I remember loneliness.
I remember stillness.
I remember when it was still there.
I know the edge is coming.
I know it won't be there long.
I know tides rise.
I know fish drown.

THE LEVEE IS NOT AS GOOD AS AN IDEA
AS IT WAS BEFORE

We pump awhile, then we dredge awhile for
a bottleneck of barges locked in river sludge.
The saltwater intrusion is gradual so
there is no need to panic yet.

Fifty square miles lost to the Gulf every year,
and this has been murmured since at least the '80s
when a drought left fish gasping, but it's only
a potential problem until you're in trouble, said the state.
It's forgotten when the rain eases plight.

Until the rain raises waterlines, then we are troubled
and need to make up for lost time & lost wetland—
now the levee is not as good as an idea as it was before.

ALLUVIUM

The silted heart and heron
born of moon-silver fringes

skims the waterline.
Each touch, if briefly, inside

somewhere only ever. These
moments at the river's soft

mouth are geographically young
and unfolding, always.

A drainage pipe yields alluvial
runoff decorating the ditch

beside the cane field.
The heron extends its wings

for another flight. See?
An unfolding, always.

GEOGRAPHIES

I.

My tongue has come to know the thistle and its pairing with
vinegar and pepper and the itch surrounding watery eyes
upon bringing goldenrod up to the nose.

I have exhausted all I have to say and I have known so little
here—how the river came to be locked in place is just a story
told over plate lunches. I know no more and no less.

II.

The poem, yes, the poem, roams where unsweetened
callings demand. It traverses the back porch freshly
washed after gutting sac a lait, the flat bottom of
the pirogue drying beside the pond, the cow tongue
stewing in the Christmas lunch Magnalite, and I
have rewritten the ending sentence because I do not
want to go there. Not right now. Not with the house
in its current state after the storm, not with the port
being placed within the body for treatment. See, the
port is debated and delegated. The port is intentional.

III.

A man canoed the entirety of the Mississippi River and feared the might
of barges and ocean liners when he neared Venice. Suddenly, I am docked
watching the bridge open over Bayou Dularge as a tugboat blasts its carnival
horn upon my request. It is easy to be dwarfed as a child, easy to be made small
when a category five has a width of 300 miles. It is flatland here. I pretend
distant clouds are mountainscapes.   We are in search of our size.

FARTHER FROM THE BAYOU
THAN I'D IMAGINE COMFORTABLE,

An alligator basks its osteoderms in my childhood back yard
as my mother and I pull into the driveway. It must have been
quite the walk, webbed claws heavy with mud, to make its way
to open grass. I remember the groceries in the back seat
held a roast and petite pois peas for gravy making.
I hadn't yet learned how to make a roux, but I
knew what the smell meant and still do, though meaning
changes through the years until I feel homesick in
grocery store parking lots like an alligator far from water.

GET YOUR GENERATORS HERE

& I don't have to tell you why / you already know / 'tis the season / of hot air / of flood zones / of pressure washing the maps / our neighbor has the best house for hunkering / down / not quite drowning / algae blooms red tides / don't open the fridge / leave the tub filled / fallen trees over driveways / only driveways / thank god / my grandmother's pots in the attic / catching rainwater / catching prayers / baptismal flooding / born again waterlines / rotten floor / what's the point of scrubbing the baseboards

THOUGHTS FROM HURRICANE SEASON

Somehow, the sun still lingers high in the evening light skimming
the tops of loblolly pines leaning to the right hand of the father.

Outside the open window, a chiffon curtain standing still like a ghost, the
mosquito truck hums by on the street and my heart reverberates as that chemical

mist dances into bushes and front porch screens settling nicely into the contours
of rocking chairs. Summer greenery engulfs all that is living and wet bark

fills in the negative space between ground and treetops. A stagnant lake
sweats under algae blooms and mosquitoes brush the water's surface.

Deep beyond the horizon line, where the stomach drops over water
so frighteningly emptied, violet clouds gather and rub hands.

Not far down the road, blue tarps line the roofs of houses,
and there is so little distance from this year to last.

IN WHICH WE WAIT IT OUT

All this leaving,
all this closing the door
and watching your step
on the way out.

You duck your head
and shield flyaway hairs
from a soaking sky
so lilac quiet.

All this passing away
within 24 hours of each
other while we stand and
watch. How embarrassing

for us. So awkwardly
alive while the body
returns to the ground,
but not too deep

for fear the water will
too quickly rot away
what is left and
leaving.

THE BEST STOP
Open every day, 6 a.m. – 8 p.m.

Grit on the meatery shelves
Holy Trinity to the side
Mary awaits outside on the jagged
Curb welcoming hungry baskets

A cowboy hat peeks above the
Canned tomatoes and the aisles
Have post church goers
Collecting their boudin

An interstate cuts across
The prairie lands filled
With switchgrass and roadside kill
Bless us, O Lord, and these Thy gifts

DRIVING AWAY FROM HOME ONCE AGAIN

Except I'm sitting on I-10 westbound in deadlocked traffic
with heat blending the roadway into the sky and exhaust
fuming in the back of my mind.

I see the car ahead of me strapped down an ice chest
filled with the contents of their fridge and freezer,
and I hope I don't come home to rotting food, or rather,

I hope it is only rotting food that comprises my loss.
Maybe I should have known better. Maybe I should
have stayed, because no one can tell just how long

we will be gone. A feeling wells in my chest of
having done this recently. From the top of the
Horace-Wilkinson Bridge I look downriver

and pray that what is to come swiftly moves
through us not lingering behind for drinks after
dinner. *Hit easy, hit easy, hit easy.*

IDA, 23

I must have been the only car headed east,
the only fool headed toward the dirty side
of the storm. How did you come to be named?

       My grandmother can't remember why she
       left their home, but she knows which way
       those winds turn to extend breath upon us.

We sit around the TV and watch your temper
build for days over places where water is clear—
everything breathes when you move through.

       Garage doors expand and contract like the cragged
       animal body of a horse and trees bow for prayer
       of a swift passing and no water lines.

LAKE ROAD, MARCH

There's a gas station on the corner
of Main St. and Hwy 22 with rusted
signs and glass coke bottles on shelves.

I found love in a cherry Icee there at River's
mouth where I swam as a child
and power lines crochet the horizon.

Take a seat here, for a minute or two,
breathe in the gnats and remember
the older couple form Germany traveling

in a camper half the size of my thumb.
Her round cheeks and his bloated belly
hinted at a fried catfish lunch.

This is the land of the sinking, I say,
where cattails wash themselves away
after a warm night like soap suds
on weathered palms.

THOUGHTS FROM LAST JUNE

We bobble like buoys across the slip
traversing pasta water toward
a gas station and somewhere
Fleetwood Mac plays on weather-worn radios.
It's a secondhand boat but the third
in my lifetime. Chopped water
knocks upon the pontoons
all *swoosh* and *galoosh*
and a gull harmonizes with that
all-too-signature sound of chords—
no church choir here but a beer can
be holy sweating in a cup holder, aluminum
singing its rattle in afternoon sun.
Chips sandwiched between Leidenheimer,
sunscreen taints each bite,
that afternoon thunderstorm creeps
along the horizon setting the tone
for a nap between sandy sheets,
and the smell of gasoline lingers
in a sun
burnt nose.

WE DROWNED THE OYSTERS THIS YEAR

And so I wish dawn meant birth.
If there's something to love,
it's the clack of the train on the cane field's edge.

Rocking chairs etch their names into wooden
floorboards with each passing quake.
Paint fades yellow and wood rots to the seasons.

Did you hear the oysters drowned this year?
They opened the spillway to move the river,
and somehow we will pass in its wake.

On the edge of the marsh,
where the mud smells of sulfur,
you can find the dying.

With dawn comes the surge of storms.

MIRED

Sometimes we have to give ourselves over
        to what the body softly chases

like a dog seeking out the windblown weeds.
        All night knows is of the dark and dazzling

light collapsed to the earth stuck in the ditches.
        Mud tickles the toes of decayed stars.

Give yourself over to the swampy earth—
        know it'll devour you whole,

and pass you through the earth's bowels
        digested and wholly new. Holy, holy.

I dance in sparkling mists hugging the tops
        of cypress trees until the grit between my toes

weighs me down. I am dragged to the mired
        bottom and my vocal cords rub together

and I croak. I croak like a child's fairytale frog
        begging the princess for attention

until the marshy fringe appears and kisses
        my sweating cheek. I am a saint. I am silt.

I am a proverbial arm reaching for the moon
        and whatever she can offer me.

MAUREPAS

There is little known here
        Where the earth chews slowly
                Always some moment between

life and decay. A foot slips into
        dark waters while playing
                And shadows stretch across

slow moving rivers of another
        World present before us.
                We are only visitors

in this agitated land, always
        Rotting from the inside out.
                This is no garden

for the living, only ghosts
        Willing to share a bite.
                The earth chews petroleum

slowly as though natural
        gas aids the quick living
                quick loving quick

to love and lose
        All too soon
                in the stretching shadows

of the bayou below
        where the agitated land
                rots from the inside out.

BAIT

A bright memory highlights
the corners of my eyes

and I am nine years old
somewhere on a dock again.

The scales of fish glint beneath
sepia waters on a calm day.

My grandmother baits her hook, carefully
curving the shrimp along the J

before casting her line into the
waters below. Egrets dust the

horizon line, and pelicans adorn
the posts of piers like ornaments.

A cold beer sits in her cupholder
and no worries flush our cheeks yet.

Nothing is quite yet lost.

MAGNALITE POT
8 Qts / 7.5 Liter

Scorched bottom seen a roux or two
Mama keeps it stored below the drawers

That house miscellaneous coupons
The same drawers my curious fingers

Would root through as a bored child
Before we moved when the first flood

Crept through the back yard and up the porch
Fleur de Lis all swoops embossed on the silver

Underside and the mind remembers gold
But it's really the toasted stains of red gravy and roux

The color of peanut butter (a little darker) because that's how
Mama taught it—grab a chair and keep stirring

Smelling like the three days of fall when
The windows stayed open and the air felt dry

EVACUATION
After "Hurricane Parties" by Cody Smith

On the northeast side of the storm
stuck just south of I-10.

Mom rings on the phone to fill the tank,
as Dad reminds me to park on high grounds.

Water bottles in the freezer.
Ice chest on standby.

Batteries, MREs,
and generators hum.

This isn't the first storm
I've weathered on my own.

We do these things, you see.
Someone closes the spillway.

Then we rearrange the patio plants,
terracotta pots lining the walls.

Neighbors board up
the house's shutters.

We drink in the rain together,
and talk about future plans

in celebration of what is to come,
and what is to pass.

FOR DIANA & EMMETT

It's easy to start with the potatoes growing firm and round in the blackened ear
a beloved tractor ride carrying a bride and her ensemble over knuckled ground

or the Christmas steaks a step above well done stacked orderly in the Magnalite
making its debut once again. We share laughs through toughened chews.

A cramped kitchen with great grandchildren toddling over tile floor
that lined my own home's floor, bare feet coming to know the coolness
all too well after a walk over July's blacktop.

A shared driveway because that highway goes fast past a place taking its time
and a shed in the back littered with tools my father knows best.

The bedroom has purple pansies on the bedspread—a subtle yellow peeking
through. Yes, yes, Go Tigers everywhere we can.

Joined hands around the table,
Bless us, O Lord, and these thy gifts.

A TWITTER USER POSTS A PHOTO
AFTER IDA

And in it is a pink dumpster with noon thirty light
shining straight down on a blue tarp laying atop
a heap of branches. Black trash bags line the street

behind the dumpster filled with cleaned-out fridges.
Remnants of water puddle-line the potholes. Power
lines stand useless in the background. But here,

here in this pink dumpster, is the body of an alligator.
Heaping tail slumped over the front of the bin and
a red hibiscus fully in bloom laying on top.

I guess the alligator fucked around and found out.
Is this a lyric from The House of the Rising Sun?
I cannot decipher the metaphor here.

MY FATHER PREFERS SHUCKING OYSTERS
TO EATING THEM

maybe it's an affinity for hard work and calloused hands

beers converge in the belly like rivers tickling the lake's edge

melted butter, garlic, and specks of parsley swirl together

brushed atop the soft and glistening flesh nestled in a half shell

flames of a grill growing wild and hot against winter air

a wooden swing splinters against my thighs, its color

long faded to a weathered grey and I imagine it

being built some distant day ago in a much smaller town

with a much younger grandfather when the smell of char

grilled oysters brings me elsewhere

and I am unsure of where I am going

THOUGHTS FROM LAKE MARTIN

That infant green peeps through on oakened
branches and roseate spoonbills wade
next to rainbow oil spilled from motors

of eager fishermen. Stopped cars align themselves
against the ditch; clear fishing line tangles
itself in cypress needles like rosaries woven

between praying fingers. A split brown bottle
glistens unwholly against the ground. Kudzu pervades
that empty house as binoculars hang from onlookers'

necks, and the lid of a blue cooler lays crooked and open
while largemouth bass gasp over bait shack ice—frightening,
that awful red of gills all membrane and sponge.

B. 1947

The navel oranges aren't ready for picking quite yet, and your grandfather got swept away planting lemon trees. Lots o' vegetables in the garden this year. Your great grandmother used to say *veggie-tables*. *Too many sill-ah-bulls*, she'd say. My parents were good people; they were just stupid people. Didn't know how to practice birth control. Not that anyone at that time was outwardly interested. Seven children. Seven. And here I am, the oldest, raising all that came next. I could've killed my brother, you know. Sheer resentment. A great penis swings between the legs and suddenly you don't have to change a damn diaper. Things change, people grow, time goes on and you have kids of your own. You can still change your mind, you know.

YOU ARE HERE

You-are-here finds me circled in the corner
of the map, of the edge, of sunken shoreline, of sediment
falling off continental shelves like people leaving
an empty parish. It's how ghost towns unspool

at the end of the school year. It's how storm season
closes in on two-year-old blue tarped roofs. It's how
we cough up brown water that gives and gives.
The things we lose in your wake surface up again

when waterlines rise then recede. Tombstones
resurface, mouths agape and lopsided gasping
for a breath of muggy air. It's not that tattooed cypress
trunks indicate past waterlines, but that it comes

up our sinks and floods the living room floor
and you are here standing in the wake of it all.

DELTA, REVISITED

it is February and I'm pretending
there are distant mountain lines somewhere
near so when grief saunters in like the tide
and the body can do nothing but ache
something can be found higher
than sea level and fishbowl cities

a purpling sky grows hazy on the outskirts
mountain lines shift from thing to you
back in July when I can still smell
freshly pulled crab traps all salt and pinch
as elevation disappears   and I sink
like the *kerplunk* of a slippery wedding ring

but this is all a game of pretend since February is
an honest month and August debris still lines the streets

CLOSING ENTRY

when you open   yourself to the   cold dirt   let yourself not be wary, but grateful for damp soil to soften the   toughest parts calloused on your heart.   a nameless want still lingers   behind. transformation isn't linear—it follows   no chronology other than the path   our thoughts take, revisiting the   weights of our   memories. in this sweet earth there is   so much that   winds like   poison oak on its way to the sun. confront your grief.   stand on the edge of its waters beside the   pickerelweed and let its torrents soak you. remember,   remember,   the river floods to bring new growth. confront your grief   with an open heart. the softened earth   eats away callouses on the heart. an extension of the self lives onward. be still.

AFTERTHOUGHT

I chase what is lost
and bemired;

so, what of surges
that bludgeon the last

of barrier islands
doing as water does—

taking as it takes,
and giving as it gives

formless and furied,
muddled and amiss?

OF HURRICANE SEASON

The promise of a hard hit hasn't been entirely washed away with the arrival of cooler days. Colorful infographics show notice of a disturbance deep in the belly of the Atlantic. A yellow funnel shows the bend and curve of its predicted path.

Just last year, you were in the kitchen with your grandmother. She was unsure of why she was there, but she knew which way those winds turn to extend breath upon us.

2005

You were sleeping on a mattress in the living room because upstairs was too far away. All night the boards of the house groaned with pressure. When the tv came back on, a generator humming somewhere in the background, you saw images of a city fishbowled and people praying on a roof of their home. You felt a white-hot heat on the edge of your chest.

2009

Found yourself evacuated in Mississippi at a family friend's place. This was the year you kept asking for a dog. The back yard flooded to the front porch, migrating like you do from morning to evening. Eventually, it receded back into the river > back into the lake > back into the marsh > back into the Gulf.

Like these things, people try to predict you, but you stay when told to leave. You drive on an open interstate headed toward the dirty side of the storm—an ice chest strapped to your back bumper. You pray downriver while crossing the Mississippi, but not like how Mama taught you. You pray of a swift passing and no waterlines.

You watch me build for days where waters are open and clear. It's the way you dishevel yourselves for me. Throw the coat on the floor, the truck in the pool. The fear of another great disaster lingers. Fear of paralysis. Fear of flood. Fear of no preparation. Fear of losing the garden. Aside from record smashing death and destruction, the tomatoes will return next season. Storm toll rises; relief rolls in.

Easy to say I am windblown and rain ridden. Sopping wet with littered leftovers. Little known here the earth chews slowly, always somewhere between life and decay. Deep water horizon lines withstanding this bandwidth. Just a moment in the Atlantic and some-forever-elsewhere in the books.

Before this thing hit, we boarded up the house's shutters. We filled the bathtub with water, the car with gas. The neighbors walked over, and we made a toast. No one knew it would be four days of life and sensational headlines. Barrier islands took the first of it, now gone. Searchers trudge into desolation. The waters stop rising, but only because they equalized with the lake. "Faith, prayer were the keys," they say.

A suppressed twinge of excitement runs up the length of your forearms, from the tip of your index finger to the muscular socket at your shoulder blade. You bury it underneath the weight of packing and leaving. When the air feels still and the trees go quiet, a sense of smallness settles in. There is bewilderment in your eyes and fear somewhere on the roof of your mouth. Anticipation colors the next 48 hours.

You like to imagine a rope is tied around the river's waist, and from here you gently suggest a new line of flow that avoids your back yard. You see, when the river floods to bring new growth, you lose the tomatoes. Let the river lead and lose the tomatoes. Let the river lead and bend in its wake. The books say *be water.* Sink like a leaden fish weight.

Headed east on an empty stretch of interstate, while the westbound traffic sits in a deadlock. *I have always been a storm*, sings the radio. You pray you don't bring the storm with you, but what is done is done. Military vehicles bring sandbags, MREs, generators, and flashlights somewhere east. Somewhere you're headed. You can't change even an afternoon shower. A trickle.

a squall can produce spiraled rain bands calling upon something horizontal in the atmosphere unseen and unfelt until activated by water with ultra-efficiency to soak and baptize / until inflow energizes the coiling, rotation magnetizes and utilizes metal specks in the air wind-eroding from offshore rigs / once air pressure equalizes, the eyewall dissipates into freshly laid mulch / meanwhile, ensembles choir together and predict paths of outcome

Flood water crept up onto the dock. The river flowed in reverse inland from the estuary with the oncoming storm. Preparation underway. Storm duty. Disaster Area. Homes stricken. Take to the water and give away again. Purchase batteries. Scramble into action. Wait it out. Ride it out. Count your blessings. Storm toll rises. Many structures had vanished. But not the people.

A tracheal hum from the bottom of the Gulf. Patio furniture in the pool. Concrete buildings. Zoom out on the spaghetti model—it's not just us in this. *It passed through quick. Worst of it rolled through during the night.*

overturned terracotta pot cracked on the edges all mosaic and shambles dirt blown across the concrete dark grey and saturated with water that came up from the Gulf deep brown it sits stagnant below the treeline a closer inspection shows maggots and centipedes swirling at its surface likely wondering what brought water to dry ground if maggots and centipedes do wonder about their current circumstances pause before you swallow / hands to the throat signifies choking / hands to the sky signifies the lost among wreckage of a home / torn away in two years' time / keep the leash around the river and lead it softly / candy citrus peels during / note the lemons returned on the trees / a seed caught in the throat / hands to the throat signifies choking / water is the most destructive force on the earth a generator clicks on in the background gasoline moan electric the smell of sulfur in the atmosphere everything is some sort of wet and dampened even the heart puddles in a chest cavity after a downpour like that people say torrential before they say downpour people say amen after a prayer answered mumbled lips and frantic kiss to the cross it fell off the wall in all that wind

cold soup from the can tastes metallic like a split lip finger cut on the can's tin toss in the garbage and keep the lid strapped down animals have a way of being hungry well into the night and day of the third week without power wondering when maps will be redrawn and insurance distributed sunken bridge still intact but somehow fell below the surface of water like the slippery *kerplunk* of a wedding ring on thin fingers some distant winter day when all we have is this heat in our bellies spooning from pots in the attic catching rainwater wondering whether tidal pools will eventually run dry there is silt at the end of the Mississippi we lift our eyes while passing through high water hell raised

Except for standing water in fields, the occasional downed cedar or oak, initial caution seemed the usual. In spite of what we have suffered, we have been spared, some say on high ground. Thin strips of land remain along the edge. A signpost in Cocodrie reads, "Welcome to the End of the World." An entrance.

don't trip / stay away from high water / park on higher ground / wonder why / avoid the curiosities / a shovel won't do you too good / celebrate when you can / fill the belly with rice and gravy / say a rosary / ask forgiveness / forget what you said when the power went out

ACKNOWLEDGMENTS

I would like to extend a huge thank you to the literary journals that first published a selection of these poems.

"Ida, 23" and "Geographies," Belle Point Press: *Mid/South Anthology* (2022)
"Driving Away from Home Once Again" and "Thoughts from Hurricane Season," *Deep South Magazine* (2022)
"Magnalite Pot," *Eco Theo Review* (2022)
"Alluvium," *Susurrus* (2021)
"Maurepas" and "Mired," *Moss Puppy Magazine* (2021)
"A Twitter User Posts a Photo after Ida," *Tilted House* (2021)
"Delta," *The Tide Rises Journal* (2021)
"Closing Entry," *The Madrigal* (2021)
"Founded in Freshwater, Birthed to the Brackish," *Glass Mountain* (2020)

I should also like to thank my dear family for the endless love and support.

MADELINE TROSCLAIR-ROTOLO is a poet from Southeast Louisiana. She holds a masters of English in creative writing from the University of Louisiana at Lafayette. With an emphasis on ecological poetry, her work has been featured in *Susurrus Magazine, The Tide Rises Journal, Tilted House*, and *EcoTheo Review*. *Bottomlands* is her first full-length poetry collection. She is fond of muddy rivers, garlic, and warm light.

Bottomlands
was designed, edited, and typeset by
Belle Point Press in Fort Smith, Arkansas.

The text is set in Adobe Caslon Pro.
Titles are set in Source Sans.

The mission of Belle Point Press is to celebrate the
literary culture and community
of the American Mid-South:
all its paradoxes and contradictions,
all the ways it gets us home.
Visit us at
www.bellepointpress.com.

Fort Smith, Arkansas

CPSIA information can be obtained
at www.ICGtesting.com
Printed in the USA
BVHW031317120423
662139BV00003B/3